Loud Louie

By Sheila Sweeny Higginson
Based on the episode written by Noelle Wright
Illustrated by Alan Batson

WWW.ABDOPUBLISHING.COM

Reinforced library bound edition published in 2015 by Spotlight, a division of ABDO
PO Box 398166, Minneapolis, Minnesota 55439. Spotlight produces high-quality reinforced library
bound editions for schools and libraries. Published by agreement with Disney Enterprises, Inc.

Printed in the United States of America, North Mankato, Minnesota.
052014   072014

DISNE**P** PRESS   THIS BOOK CONTAINS
RECYCLED MATERIALS

LIBRARY OF CONGRESS CATALOGING-IN-PUBLICATION DATA

This title was previously cataloged with the following information:

Higginson, Sheila Sweeny, 1966-
 Doc McStuffins: Loud Louie / Sheila Sweeny Higginson ; based on the episode written by Noelle
Wright; illustrated by Alan Batson.
   p. cm. -- (World of reading. Level Pre-1)
Summary: "Louie the cell phone needs to learn when to use his inside voice."
1. Girls--Juvenile fiction. 2. Toys--Juvenile fiction. 3. Courtesy--Juvenile fiction. I. Batson, Alan, ill. II.
Wright, Noelle. III. Title. IV. Series. V. Doc McStuffins (Television program)
[E]--dc23

                    2012285596

978-1-61479-244-4 (Reinforced Library Bound Edition)

Spotlight
A Division of ABDO
www.abdopublishing.com

 bounces a  to .
Doc   ball   Stuffy

"Oops!" he says as it lands

in the .
       toy box

A noise comes from the  toy box.
" Doc!" he says. "There's something big and loud in there!"

3

 goes over to the .

Doc   toy box

"Hello!" a voice says. "Want to

come out and play?"

4

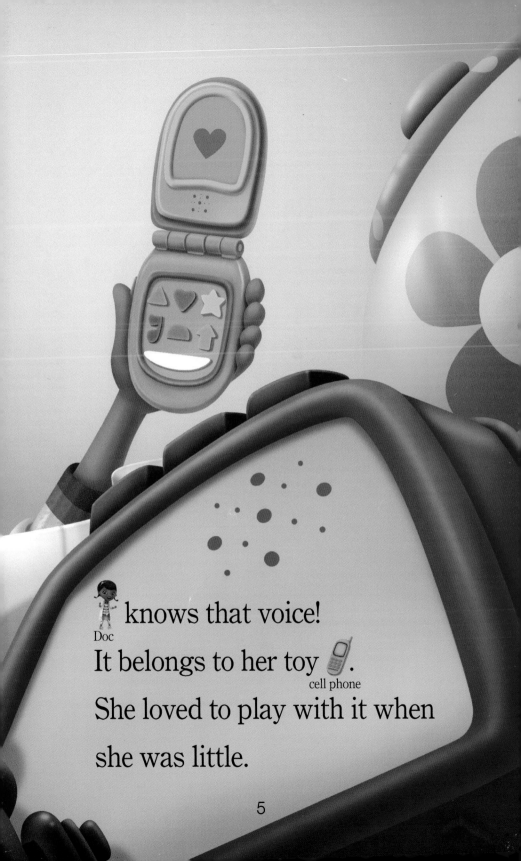

 knows that voice!

It belongs to her toy .

cell phone

She loved to play with it when

she was little.

5

 presses a button on the .
Doc   cell phone
"Leave a message after the beep,"
it says.

Doc's stethoscope begins to glow.
Then the cell phone comes to life!
"HI Doc!" it yells loudly.

7

"Hi, ," says. "It's great to

Louie   Doc

see you!"

hears a knock on the .

Doc   door

"Toys, go stuffed," she says.

8

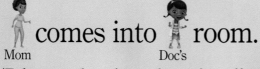 comes into room.

Mom Doc's

"I heard a loud voice," she says.

"Oh, you heard this," says.

Doc

9

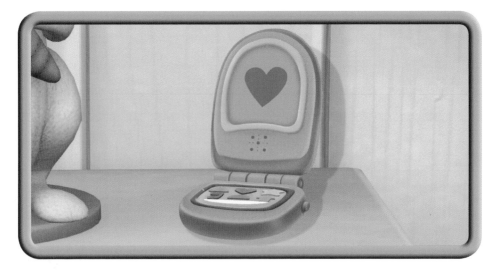

It's time for bed.
 tucks into [bed].

Mom   Doc   bed

She puts [Louie] on the table.

Louie

Then she turns out the [light].

light

After  leaves, Louie yells,
"GOOD NIGHT!"

"He sure is loud," says Lambie.

"He's just excited," Doc says.

11

is the first to wake up the
Louie
next morning.

"HEY!" he yells. "ARE YOU

GUYS AWAKE?"

"We are now," says .
"Want to come play in the clinic
with us today?" she asks.
"BOY, DO I!" says too loudly.

13

 takes  to the clinic.
Doc Louie

 meets all her friends.
Louie

"Let's show  how we play
Louie

hide-and-go-seek!"  says.
Stuffy

 starts to count. The toys hide.
"SHE'LL NEVER FIND ME
HERE!"  yells from a bin.
"Hi, ," says .

15

"UH-OH,"  says. "WAS I LOUD?"
Louie

"Too loud for hide-and-go-seek,"
 says with a giggle.
Doc

"BUT I'M NOT TRYING
TO TALK LOUD," says .
 wonders if he is broken.

 takes a close look at .

Doc Louie

 gets worried.

Louie

"Don't worry,"  says. "I'm the

Doc

best doctor around for toys."

It's time for  checkup.

listens to his .

She presses all his buttons.

 Louie opens his mouth wide and says, "AAAAAHHHH." Doc holds her ears.

"I have a diagnosis,"  says.
"You have a case of Superlouditis!"

 hands a book to . "Tell it to the Big Book of Boo-Boos,"  says.

Hallie

Doc

Hallie

22

"Something is wrong with your volume buttons," 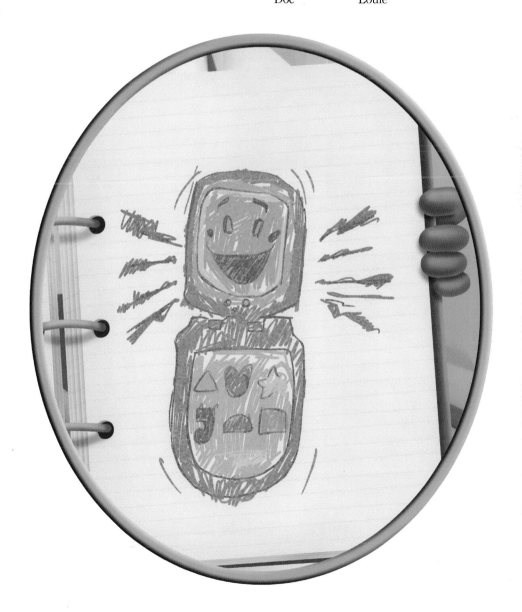 tells .

Doc   Louie

The  button is stuck.
 takes a closer look.

up

Doc

"Something is stuck,"  says.
Doc

She gets ✎ and pulls a sticker out.
tweezers

Then she turns 📱 volume down.
Louie's

25

"Thanks,"  says in a soft voice.
_{Louie}

"Your volume button works now!

We should test it out," says.
_{Doc}

"Let's play telephone," says .
_{Lambie}

26

![Doc] explains the rules to ![Louie].
Doc   Louie

Everyone sits in a ⭕.
                   circle

Then they whisper a message

from person to person.

The last person says it out loud.
"Remember to whisper,"  says.

Doc

They start the game.
But  still talks too loud.

Louie

28

"You have to use your inside voice, 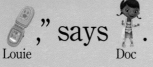," says 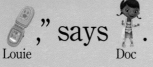.

Louie   Doc

29

starts the game again.

Stuffy

The message goes around the .

circle

 gets the message.

Louie

This time, he uses his inside voice.

whispers the message to . Louie Lambie

"You did it," says . Doc

tells her friends the message. Lambie

"You need a cuddle."

 has a telephone message for you.
Louie
Will you whisper it to a friend?